Monty
and friends
save
Christmas

Story by M.T. Sanders

Illustrations by Zoe Saunders

To Jennifer
Love from
Monty • Cookie

First edition published 2018 by 2QT Limited (Publishing).
Settle, North Yorkshire, BD24 9RH. United Kingdom.

Copyright © M.T. Sanders 2018.

Illustrations by Zoe Saunders.

Printed in Great Britain by IngramSparks.

A CIP catalogue record for this book is available from the British Library.

ISBN 978-1-912014-41-5

Dedications

This book is dedicated to all of the beautiful friends
we have loved and lost.

They are always in our hearts, thoughts and stories.

Here's to the magic of Christmas

and the power of our memories.

'Twas the eve before Christmas, on a cold winter's night, streets deserted and still, pavements frosty and white.

The shops were now closed, all the customers gone,
the quiet only broken as the church bell struck one.

Our house was all silent apart from dad snoring,
as he dreamt of the presents he'd get in the morning.
Could it be a red sports car or a hooge new TV?
Most likely just socks, left for him by the tree.

The spangles were off in a world of their own,
where Bailey occasionally shared the stag bones,
where the round man in red
brought them nice things to eat,
maybe horse and fox poo as a Christmas Day treat!

Mini-hoomans were asleep with a threat of no toys,
If they woke in the night, even if they heard noise.
So peace and tranquility ran all through the house.
But the creature to stir first wasn't a mouse...

For out in the garden there arose such a clatter,

that I jumped from my bed
to see what was the matter...

Cookie had managed to open the door,
and was **battering** Santa with a hooge hairy paw!

She thought it was Dad dressed up like the main man.

But Santa was scared
and the reindeers, they ran!

Santa lay there disheveled in his red and white clobber,
with paw prints and scuff marks and covered in slobber.

Rudolph and friends had immediately fled.
The sight of this creature had filled them with dread.
But the night was not over, there was work left to do.
The sled needed pulling, it needed a crew.

The whole world was waiting for Santa's arrival;
someone needed to help with the big day's survival.
It needed to happen fast, that was for sure.
So I took two steps forward and held up my paw.

'I'll do it', I said, 'and I have a great team.
We'll deliver the presents - it's a newfydoof's dream.
But pulling is one thing and flying's another,
we may need some help, there's some distance to cover.'

Santa just smiled and said, 'I can help.'
He pulled out his mobile and dialed up an elf.
'We need magic dust delivered NOW to Wigwam,
Monty is getting us out of a jam...'

So the dust it arrived, and we waited to go,
and just at that moment it started to snow.
Two newfydoofs, three spangles and Santa all ready.
We started to rise, so I called out 'KEEP STEADY!'

Up we went quickly and the climb carried on,
'til we looked for the ground and saw it had gone.

Then when we were high, Santa started to call
'Dash away! Dash away! Dash away all!'

We flew through the night it was really good fun,
but that sled filled with presents
weighed more than a tonne.

We could pull it no longer, and we began to go down.
We were miles from anywhere, with no sign of a town.

It was more crashing than landing;
we came down with a thud...

We were all firmly bogged down in a field full of mud.

It appeared that we'd finally ran out of luck.
The sled and its contents were totally stuck!

We pushed and we pulled but it budged not an inch,
and sleds built for reindeer don't come with a winch.
Santa sat glumly with his head in his hands,
and thought of those children in faraway lands.

They would wake with no presents
and the magic would die,
we needed a way for this vehicle to fly.
I thought and I thought but I'd ran out of ideas.
All I could think of was small hooman's tears...

When all of a sudden from the darkness, a light.
It was dim in the distance but soon glowed so bright.
We shielded our eyes as it became clearer,
then a rainbow emerged and got nearer and nearer

Right in the centre was a gate, fine and gold,
and I think then I knew from the stories of old.
The gate opened slowly, and we peered through the mist.
And that's when I realised, this place DID exist...

A large wooden bridge crossed a shimmering stream,
and I have to admit it felt just like a dream.
The night air was filled with the thudding of paws,
and hundreds of dogs rushed out through the doors.

The well-loved and faithful had returned for one day.
They surrounded the sled and pointed the way.
All breeds, shapes and sizes prepared for the pull,
and the sled moved with ease even though it was full.

We rose through the air faster with help at hand,
into the night sky, way beneath was the land.
No dust here was needed, because the magical thing
was the rainbow-bridge dogs already had wings!

We all pulled together and worked all through the night,
from country to country until it got light,
delivering presents to those good girls and boys,
who would wake in the morning to their
Christmas Day toys.

At last it was light and the job was complete.
We could all go back home and get something to eat.
Our special helpers left and we all said goodbye,
and headed back home through the early dawn sky.

When we all got back home Santa got us together,
and said what we'd done was so kind and so clever.
He said that our friends had returned to their life,
forever running and playing with no trouble or strife.

We were all overwhelmed and so privileged,
to have been helped by our pals
from across rainbow bridge.
Christmas day had been saved,
that was such a hooge feat!

Surely Santa would be handing out newfydoof treats?

Just then, he was gone. Where he went wasn't clear,
but we think he went looking for his missing reindeer.
We all wandered over and crept back into the house.
And that was the tale of how we all saved Christmas.

A little while later
I awoke to see Dad.

He said, 'We were worried.
Are you OK, old lad?'

He said I'd made noises
he thought in my sleep.

I'll let him believe that, and our secret I'll keep.

Other books available by the author ...

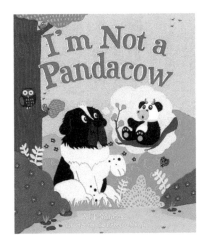

A delightful story about Monty, a huge Newfoundland puppy, and his journey to find out what he is. But will asking the other dogs he meets on his travels give him the answers he wants?

By M.T. Sanders.
With illustrations by Rebecca Sharp.

ISBN 978-1-912014-73

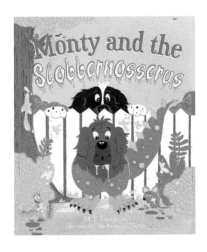

When Monty was asked to look after his new sister how hard could it be? An open gate and a fleeing mailman was just the invitation she needed.
Now it was up to Monty to save the day. So, watch out everyone it's time to run... for your raincoats.

By M.T. Sanders.
With illustrations by Rebecca Sharp.

ISBN 978-1-912014-79-8

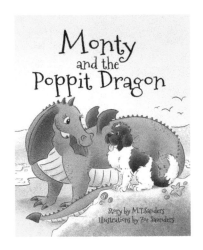

Monty, Cookie and the spangles are off on their holidays to sunny Pembrokeshire and the beautiful beach at Poppit Sands. In a cave they meet a new friend, the Poppit Dragon, who is sad because she can't fly. Can Monty and the gang save the day?

By M.T. Sanders.
With illustrations by Zoe Saunders.

ISBN 978-1-912014-06-4

Other books available by the illustrator ...

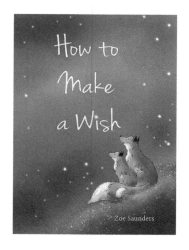

Come on a journey through the countryside as Big Red Fox teaches Little Red Fox how to make wishes. A dreamy children's story with beautiful illustrations, and a heartwarming ending that will leave children feeling loved and cherished, How to Make a Wish is perfect bedtime reading for your little cubs.

By Zoe Saunders.
ISBN 978-1-78808-0385

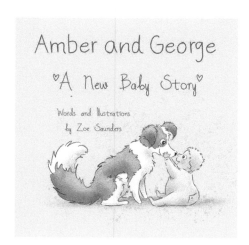

Amber is the dog who has it all. She has a lovely house, a big garden, lots of toys, and she goes for long walks every day. Then one day everything changes. A little baby called George turns Amber's perfect world upside down. But all it takes is a little time and patience for friendship and love to grow.

By Zoe Saunders.
ISBN 978-1-78926-0885

High up in the mountains, far above the clouds, where the Earth meets the sky, there lived a lonely dragon. The dragon embarks on a great journey travelling far and wide in search of a friend, another dragon, just like her. And in the end, she does find true friendship, but not quite in the way she imagined.

By Zoe Saunders.
ISBN 978-1-9164352-0-9

Lightning Source UK Ltd.
Milton Keynes UK
UKHW052124131019
351530UK00001B/2/P